THE CONSUL

BY

RICHARD HARDING DAVIS

British Library Cataloguing-in-Publication Data
A catalogue record for this book is available from the
British Library

Richard Harding Davis

Richard Harding Davis was born on 18th April 1864, in Philadelphia, Pennsylvania. He was the son of two writers, Rebecca Harding Davis (a prominent author), and Lemuel Clarke Davis (a journalist and editor of the Philadelphia Public Ledger).

Davis attended Lehigh University and Johns Hopkins University, but was asked to leave both due to neglecting his studies in favour socialising. With some help from his father, Davis was able to find a position as a journalist at the Philadelphia Record, but was soon fired from the post. He then spent a short time at the Philadelphia Press before moving to the New York Evening Sun, where he became a controversial figure, writing on subjects such as execution, abortion, and suicide. He went on to edit Harper's Weekly and write for the New York Herald, The Times, and Scribner's Magazine.

During the Second Boer War in South Africa, Davis was a leading correspondent of the conflict. He saw the war first-hand from both parties perspectives and documented it in his publication With Both Armies (1900). Later in his career he wrote a story about his experience on a United States Navy ship that shelled Cuba as part of the Battle of Santiago de Cuba. His article made the headlines and prompted the

Navy to refuse to allow reporters aboard their vessels for the remainder of the war.

He wrote widely from locations such as the Caribbean, Central America, and even from the perspective of the Japanese forces during the Russo-Japanese War. He also covered the Salonika Front in the First World War, where he spent a time detained by the Germans on suspicion of being a spy.

Davis married twice, first to Cecil Clark in 1899, and then to Bessie McCoy in 1912, with whom he had one daughter. Davis died following a heart attack on 11th April, 1916, at the age of 51.

For over forty years, in one part of the world or another, old man Marshall had, served his country as a United States consul. He had been appointed by Lincoln. For a quarter of a century that fact was his distinction. It was now his epitaph. But in former years, as each new administration succeeded the old, it had again and again saved his official head. When victorious and voracious place-hunters, searching the map of the world for spoils, dug out his hiding-place and demanded his consular sign as a reward for a younger and more aggressive party worker, the ghost of the dead President protected him. In the State Department, Marshall had become a tradition. "You can't touch Him!" the State Department would say; "why, HE was appointed by Lincoln!" Secretly, for this weapon against the hungry headhunters, the department was infinitely grateful. Old man Marshall was a consul after its own heart. Like a soldier, he was obedient, disciplined; wherever he was sent, there, without question, he would go. Never against exile, against ill-health, against climate did he make complaint. Nor when he was moved on and down to make way for some ne'er-do-well with influence, with a brother-in-law in the Senate, with a cousin owning a newspaper, with rich relatives who desired him to drink himself to death at the expense of the government rather than at their own, did old man Marshall point to his record as a claim for more just treatment.

And it had been an excellent record. His official reports, in a quaint, stately hand, were models of English; full of information, intelligent, valuable, well observed. And those few of his countrymen, who stumbled upon him in the out-of-the-world places to which of late he had been banished, wrote of him to the department in terms of admiration and awe. Never had he or his friends petitioned for promotion, until it was at last apparent that, save for his record and the memory of his dead patron, he had no friends. But, still in the department the tradition held and, though he was not advanced, he was not dismissed.

"If that old man's been feeding from the public trough ever since the Civil War," protested a "practical" politician, "it seems to me, Mr. Secretary, that he's about had his share. Ain't it time he give some one else a bite? Some of us that has, done the work, that has borne the brunt——"

"This place he now holds," interrupted the Secretary of State suavely, "is one hardly commensurate with services like yours. I can't pronounce the name of it, and I'm not sure just where it is, but I see that, of the last six consuls we sent there, three resigned within a month and the other three died of yellow-fever. Still, if you insist——"

The practical politician reconsidered hastily. "I'm not the sort," he protested, "to turn out a man appointed by our martyred President. Besides, he's so old now, if the fever don't catch him, he'll die of old age, anyway."

The Secretary coughed uncomfortably. "And they say," he murmured, "republics are ungrateful."

"I don't quite get that," said the practical politician.

Of Porto Banos, of the Republic of Colombia, where as consul Mr. Marshall was upholding the dignity of the United States, little could be said except that it possessed a sure harbor. When driven from the Caribbean Sea by stress of weather, the largest of ocean tramps, and even battleships, could find in its protecting arms of coral a safe shelter. But, as young Mr. Aiken, the wireless operator, pointed out, unless driven by a hurricane and the fear of death, no one ever visited it. Back of the ancient wharfs, that dated from the days when Porto Banos was a receiver of stolen goods for buccaneers and pirates, were rows of thatched huts, streets, according to the season, of dust or mud, a few iron-barred, jail-like barracks, customhouses, municipal buildings, and the whitewashed adobe houses of the consuls. The backyard of the town was a swamp. Through this at five each morning a rusty engine pulled a train of flat cars to the base of the mountains, and, if meanwhile the rails had not disappeared into the swamp, at five in the evening brought back the flat cars laden with odorous coffeesacks.

In the daily life of Porto Banos, waiting for the return of the train, and betting if it would return, was the chief interest. Each night the consuls, the foreign residents, the wireless operator, the manager of the rusty railroad met for dinner. There at the head of the long table, by virtue of his years, of his courtesy and distinguished manner, of his office, Mr. Marshall presided. Of the little band of exiles he was the chosen ruler. His rule was gentle. By force of example he had made existence in Porto Banos more possible. For women and children Porto Banos was a death-trap, and before "old man Marshall" came there had been no influence to remind the enforced bachelors of other days.

They had lost interest, had grown lax, irritable, morose. Their white duck was seldom white. Their cheeks were unshaven. When the sun sank into the swamp and the heat still turned Porto Banos into a Turkish bath, they threw dice on the greasy tables of the Cafe Bolivar for drinks. The petty gambling led to petty quarrels; the drinks to fever. The coming of Mr. Marshall changed that. His standard of life, his tact, his worldly wisdom, his cheerful courtesy, his fastidious personal neatness shamed the younger men; the desire to please him, to, stand well in his good opinion, brought back pride and self-esteem.

The lieutenant of her Majesty's gun-boat PLOVER noted the change.

"Used to be," he exclaimed, "you couldn't get out of the Cafe Bolivar without some one sticking a knife in you; now it's a debating club. They all sit round a table and listen to an old gentleman talk world politics."

If Henry Marshall brought content to the exiles of Porto Banos, there was little in return that Porto Banos could give to him. Magazines and correspondents in six languages kept him in touch with those foreign lands in which he had represented his country, but of the country he had represented, newspapers and periodicals showed him only too clearly that in forty years it had grown away from him, had changed beyond recognition.

When last he had called at the State Department, he had been made to feel he was a man without a country, and when he visited his home town in Vermont, he was looked upon as a Rip Van Winkle. Those of his boyhood friends who were not dead had long thought of him as dead. And the sleepy, pretty village had become a bustling commercial centre. In the lanes where, as a young man, he had walked among wheatfields, trolley-cars whirled between rows of mills and factories. The children had grown to manhood, with children of their own.

Like a ghost, he searched for house after house, where once he had been made welcome, only to find in its place a towering office building. "All had gone, the old familiar faces." In vain he scanned even the shop fronts for a friendly, homelike name. Whether the fault was his, whether he would better have served his own interests than those of his government, it now was too late to determine. In his own home, he was a stranger among strangers. In the service he had so faithfully followed, rank by rank, he had been dropped, until now he, who twice had been a consul-general, was an exile, banished to a fever swamp. The great Ship of State had dropped him overside, had "marooned" him, and sailed away.

Twice a day he walked along the shell road to the Cafe Bolivar, and back again to the consulate. There, as he entered the outer office, Jose, the Colombian clerk, would rise and bow profoundly.

"Any papers for me to sign, Jose?" the consul would ask.

"Not to-day, Excellency," the clerk would reply. Then Jose would return to writing a letter to his lady-love; not that there was any-thing to tell her, but because writing on the official paper of the consulate gave him importance in his eyes, and in hers. And in the inner office the consul would continue to gaze at the empty harbor, the empty coral reefs, the empty, burning sky.

The little band of exiles were at second break fast when the wireless man came in late to announce that a Red D. boat and the island of Curacao had both reported a hurricane coming north. Also, that much concern was felt for the safety of the yacht SERAPIS. Three days before, in advance of her coming, she had sent a wireless to Wilhelmstad, asking the captain of the port to reserve a berth for her. She expected to arrive the following morning. But for forty-eight hours nothing had been heard from her, and it was believed she had been overhauled by the hurricane. Owing to the presence on board of Senator Hanley, the closest friend of the new President, the man who had made him president, much concern was felt at Washington. To try to pick her up by wireless, the gun-boat NEWARK had been ordered from Culebra, the cruiser RALEIGH, with Admiral Hardy on board, from Colon. It was possible she would seek shelter at Porto Banos. The consul was ordered to report.

As Marshall wrote out his answer, the French consul exclaimed with interest:

"He is of importance, then, this senator?" he asked. "Is it that in your country ships of war are at the service of a senator?"

Aiken, the wireless operator, grinned derisively.

"At the service of THIS senator, they are!" he answered. "They call him the 'king-maker,' the man behind the throne."

"But in your country," protested the Frenchman, "there is no throne. I thought your president was elected by the people?"

"That's what the people think," answered Aiken. "In God's country," he explained, "the trusts want a rich man in the Senate, with the same interests as their own, to represent them. They chose Hanley. He picked out of the candidates for the presidency the man he thought would help the interests. He nominated him, and the people voted for him. Hanley is what we call a 'boss.'"

The Frenchman looked inquiringly at Marshall.

"The position of the boss is the more dangerous," said Marshall gravely, "because it is unofficial, because there are no laws to curtail his powers. Men like Senator Hanley are a menace to good government. They see in public office only a reward for party workers."

"That's right," assented Aiken. "Your forty years' service, Mr. Consul, wouldn't count with Hanley. If he wanted your job, he'd throw you out as quick as he would a drunken cook."

Mr. Marshall flushed painfully, and the French consul hastened to interrupt.

"Then, let us pray," he exclaimed, with fervor, "that the hurricane has sunk the SERAPIS, and all on board."

Two hours later, the SERAPIS, showing she had met the hurricane and had come out second best, steamed into the harbor.

Her owner was young Herbert Livingstone, of Washington. He once had been in the diplomatic service, and, as minister to The Hague, wished to return to it. In order to bring this about he had subscribed liberally to the party campaign fund.

With him, among other distinguished persons, was the all-powerful Hanley. The kidnapping of Hanley for the cruise, in itself, demonstrated the ability of Livingstone as a diplomat. It was the opinion of many that it would surely lead to his appointment as a minister plenipotentiary. Livingstone was of the same opinion. He had not lived long in the nation's capital without observing the value of propinquity. How many men he knew were now paymasters, and secretaries of legation, solely because those high in the government met them daily at the Metropolitan Club, and preferred them in almost any other place. And if, after three weeks as his guest on board what the newspapers called his floating palace, the senator could refuse him even the prize, legation of Europe, there was no value in modest merit. As yet, Livingstone had not hinted at his ambition. There was no need. To a statesman of Hanley's astuteness, the largeness of Livingstone's contribution to the campaign fund was self-explanatory.

After her wrestling-match with the hurricane, all those on board the SERAPIS seemed to find in land, even in the swamp land of Porto Banos, a compelling attraction. Before the anchors hit the water, they were in the launch. On reaching shore, they made at once for the consulate. There were many cables they wished to start on their way by wireless; cables to friends, to newspapers, to the government.

Jose, the Colombian clerk, appalled by the unprecedented invasion of visitors, of visitors so distinguished, and Marshall, grateful for a chance to serve his fellow-countrymen, and especially his countrywomen, were ubiquitous, eager, indispensable. At Jose's desk the great senator, rolling his cigar between his teeth, was using, to Jose's ecstasy, Jose's own pen to write a reassuring message to the White House. At the consul's desk a beautiful creature, all in lace and pearls, was struggling to compress the very low opinion she held of a hurricane into ten words. On his knee, Henry Cairns, the banker, was inditing instructions to his Wall Street office, and upon himself Livingstone had taken the responsibility of replying to the inquiries heaped upon Marshall's desk, from many newspapers.

It was just before sunset, and Marshall produced his tea things, and the young person in pearls and lace, who was Miss Cairns, made tea for the women, and the men mixed gin and limes with tepid water. The consul apologized for proposing a toast in which they could not join. He begged to drink to those who had escaped the perils of the sea. Had they been his oldest and nearest friends, his little speech could not have been more heart-felt and sincere. To his distress, it moved one of the ladies to tears, and in embarrassment he turned to the men.

"I regret there is no ice," he said, "but you know the rule of the tropics; as soon as a ship enters port, the ice-machine bursts."

"I'll tell the steward to send you some, sir," said Livingstone, "and as long as we're here."

The senator showed his concern.

"As long as we're here?" he gasped.

"Not over two days," answered the owner nervously. "The chief says it will take all of that to get her in shape. As you ought to know, Senator, she was pretty badly mauled."

The senator gazed blankly out of the window. Beyond it lay the naked coral reefs, the empty sky, and the ragged palms of Porto Banos.

Livingstone felt that his legation was slipping from him.

"That wireless operator," he continued hastily, "tells me there is a most amusing place a few miles down the coast, Las Bocas, a sort of Coney Island, where the government people go for the summer. There's surf bathing and roulette and cafes chantants. He says there's some Spanish dancers——"

The guests of the SERAPIS exclaimed with interest; the senator smiled. To Marshall the general enthusiasm over the thought of a ride on a merry-go-round suggested that the friends of Mr. Livingstone had found their own society far from satisfying.

Greatly encouraged, Livingstone continued, with enthusiasm:

"And that wireless man said," he added, "that with the launch we can get there in half an hour. We might run down after dinner." He turned to Marshall.

"Will you join us, Mr. Consul?" he asked, "and dine with us, first?"

Marshall accepted with genuine pleasure. It had been many months since he had sat at table with his own people. But he shook his head doubtfully.

"I was wondering about Las Bocas," he explained, "if your going there might not get you in trouble at the next port. With a yacht, I think it is different, but Las Bocas is under quarantine."

There was a chorus of exclamations.

"It's not serious," Marshall explained. "There was bubonic plague there, or something like it. You would be in no danger from that. It is only that you might be held up by the regulations. Passenger steamers can't land any one who has been there at any other port of the West Indies. The English are especially strict. The Royal Mail won't even receive any one on board here without a certificate from the English consul saying he has not visited Las Bocas. For an American they would require the same guarantee from me. But I don't think the regulations extend to yachts. I will inquire. I don't wish to deprive you of any of the many pleasures of Porto Banos," he added, smiling, "but if you were refused a landing at your next port I would blame myself."

"It's all right," declared Livingstone decidedly. "It's just as you say; yachts and warships are exempt. Besides, I carry my own doctor, and if he won't give us a clean bill of health, I'll make him walk the plank. At eight, then, at dinner. I'll send the cutter for you. I can't give you a salute, Mr. Consul, but you shall have all the side boys I can muster."

Those from the yacht parted from their consul in the most friendly spirit.

"I think he's charming!" exclaimed Miss Cairns. "And did you notice his novels? They were in every language. It must be terribly lonely down here, for a man like that."

"He's the first of our consuls we've met on this trip," growled her father, "that we've caught sober."

"Sober!" exclaimed his wife indignantly.

"He's one of the Marshalls of Vermont. I asked him."

"I wonder," mused Hanley, "how much the place is worth? Hamilton, one of the new senators, has been deviling the life out of me to send his son somewhere. Says if he stays in Washington he'll disgrace the family. I should think this place would drive any man to drink himself to death in three months, and young Hamilton, from what I've seen of him, ought to be able to do it in a week. That would leave the place open for the next man."

"There's a postmaster in my State thinks he carried it." The senator smiled grimly. "He has consumption, and wants us to give him a consulship in the tropics. I'll tell him I've seen Porto Banos, and that it's just the place for him."

The senator's pleasantry was not well received. But Miss Cairns alone had the temerity to speak of what the others were thinking.

"What would become of Mr. Marshall?" she asked. The senator smiled tolerantly.

"I don't know that I was thinking of Mr. Marshall," he said. "I can't recall anything he has done for this administration. You see, Miss Cairns," he explained, in the tone of one addressing a small child, "Marshall has been abroad now for forty years, at the expense of the taxpayers. Some of us think men who have lived that long on their fellow-countrymen had better come home and get to work."

Livingstone nodded solemnly in assent. He did not wish a post abroad at the expense of the taxpayers. He was willing to pay for it. And then, with "ex-Minister" on his visiting cards, and a sense of duty well performed, for the rest of his life he could join the other expatriates in Paris.

Just before dinner, the cruiser RALEIGH having discovered the whereabouts of the SERAPIS by wireless, entered the harbor, and Admiral Hardy came to the yacht to call upon the senator, in whose behalf he had been scouring the Caribbean Seas. Having paid his respects to that personage, the admiral fell boisterously upon Marshall.

The two old gentlemen were friends of many years. They had met, officially and unofficially, in many strange parts of the world. To each the chance reunion was a piece of tremendous good fortune. And throughout dinner the guests of Livingstone, already bored with each other, found in them and their talk of former days new and delightful entertainment. So much so that when, Marshall having assured them that the local quarantine regulations did not extend to a yacht, the men departed for Las Bocas, the women insisted that he and admiral remain behind.

It was for Marshall a wondrous evening. To foregather with his old friend whom he had known since Hardy was a mad midshipman, to sit at the feet of his own charming countrywomen, to listen to their soft, modulated laughter, to note how quickly they saw that to him the evening was a great event, and with what tact each contributed to make it the more memorable; all served to wipe out the months of bitter loneliness, the stigma of failure, the sense of undeserved neglect. In the moonlight, on the cool quarter-deck, they sat, in a half-circle, each of the two friends telling tales out of school, tales of which the other was the hero or the victim, "inside" stories of great occasions, ceremonies, bombardments, unrecorded "shirt-sleeve" diplomacy.

Hardy had helped to open the Suez Canal. Marshall had assisted the Queen of Madagascar to escape from the French invaders. On the Barbary Coast Hardy had chased pirates. In Edinburgh Marshall had played chess with Carlyle. He had seen Paris in mourning in the days of the siege, Paris in terror in the days of the Commune; he had known Garibaldi, Gambetta, the younger Dumas, the creator of Pickwick.

"Do you remember that time in Tangier," the admiral urged, "when I was a midshipman, and got into the bashaw's harem?"

"Do you remember how I got you out? Marshall replied grimly.

"And," demanded Hardy, "do you remember when Adelina Patti paid a visit to the KEARSARGE at Marseilles in '65—George Dewey was our second officer—and you were bowing and backing away from her, and you backed into an open hatch, and she said 'my French isn't up to it' what was it she said?"

"I didn't hear it," said Marshall; "I was too far down the hatch."

"Do you mean the old KEARSARGE?" asked Mrs. Cairns. "Were you in the service then, Mr. Marshall?"

With loyal pride in his friend, the admiral answered for him:

"He was our consul-general at Marseilles!"

There was an uncomfortable moment. Even those denied imagination could not escape the contrast, could see in their mind's eye the great harbor of Marseilles, crowded with the shipping of the world, surrounding it the beautiful city, the rival of Paris to the north, and on the battleship the young consul-general making his bow to the young Empress of Song. And now, before their actual eyes, they saw the village of Porto Banos, a black streak in the night, a row of mud shacks, at the end of the wharf a single lantern yellow in the clear moonlight.

Later in the evening Miss Cairns led the admiral to one side.

"Admiral," she began eagerly, "tell me about your friend. Why is he here? Why don't they give him a place worthy of him? I've seen many of our representatives abroad, and I know we cannot afford to waste men like that." The girl exclaimed indignantly: "He's one of the most interesting men I've ever met! He's lived everywhere, known every one. He's a distinguished man, a cultivated man; even I can see he knows his work, that he's a diplomat, born, trained, that he's——" The admiral interrupted with a growl.

"You don't have to tell ME about Henry," he protested. "I've known Henry twenty-five years. If Henry got his deserts," he exclaimed hotly, "he wouldn't be a consul on this coral reef; he'd be a minister in Europe. Look at me! We're the same age. We started together. When Lincoln sent him to Morocco as consul, he signed my commission as a midshipman. Now I'm an admiral. Henry has twice my brains and he's been a consul-general, and he's HERE, back at the foot of the ladder!"

"Why?" demanded the girl.

"Because the navy is a service and the consular service isn't a service. Men like Senator Hanley use it to pay their debts. While Henry's been serving his country abroad, he's lost his friends, lost his 'pull.' Those politicians up at Washington have no use for him. They don't consider that a consul like Henry can make a million dollars for his countrymen. He can keep them from shipping goods where there's no market, show them where there is a market." The admiral snorted contemptuously. "You don't have to tell ME the value of a good consul. But those politicians don't consider that. They only see that he has a job worth a few hundred dollars, and they want it, and if he hasn't other politicians to protect him, they'll take it." The girl raised her head.

"Why don't you speak to the senator?" she asked. "Tell him you've known him for years, that——"

"Glad to do it!" exclaimed the admiral heartily. "It won't be the first time. But Henry mustn't know. He's too confoundedly touchy. He hates the IDEA of influence, hates men like Hanley, who abuse it. If he thought anything was given to him except on his merits, he wouldn't take it."

"Then we won't tell him," said the girl. For a moment she hesitated.

"If I spoke to Mr. Hanley," she asked, "told him what I learned to-night of Mr. Marshall, would it have any effect?"

"Don't know how it will affect Hanley," said the sailor, "but if you asked me to make anybody a consul-general, I'd make him an ambassador."

Later in the evening Hanley and Livingstone were seated alone on deck. The visit to Las Bocas had not proved amusing, but, much to Livingstone's relief, his honored guest was now in good-humor. He took his cigar from his lips, only to sip at a long cool drink. He was in a mood flatteringly confidential and communicative.

"People have the strangest idea of what I can do for them," he laughed. It was his pose to pretend he was without authority. "They believe I've only to wave a wand, and get them anything they want. I thought I'd be safe from them on board a yacht."

Livingstone, in ignorance of what was coming, squirmed apprehensively.

"But it seems," the senator went on, "I'm at the mercy of a conspiracy. The women folk want me to do something for this fellow Marshall. If they had their way, they'd send him to the Court of St. James. And old Hardy, too, tackled me about him. So did Miss Cairns. And then Marshall himself got me behind the wheel-house, and I thought he was going to tell me how good he was, too! But he didn't."

As though the joke were on himself, the senator laughed appreciatively.

"Told me, instead, that Hardy ought to be a vice-admiral."

Livingstone, also, laughed, with the satisfied air of one who cannot be tricked.

"They fixed it up between them," he explained, "each was to put in a good word for the other." He nodded eagerly. "That's what I think."

There were moments during the cruise when Senator Hanley would have found relief in dropping his host overboard. With mock deference, the older man inclined his head.

"That's what you think, is it?" he asked. "Livingstone," he added, "you certainly are a great judge of men!"

The next morning, old man Marshall woke with a lightness at his heart that had been long absent. For a moment, conscious only that he was happy, he lay between sleep and waking, frowning up at his canopy of mosquito net, trying to realize what change had come to him. Then he remembered. His old friend had returned. New friends had come into his life and welcomed him kindly. He was no longer lonely. As eager as a boy, he ran to the window. He had not been dreaming. In the harbor lay the pretty yacht, the stately, white-hulled war-ship. The flag that drooped from the stern of each caused his throat to tighten, brought warm tears to his eyes, fresh resolve to his discouraged, troubled spirit. When he knelt beside his bed, his heart poured out his thanks in gratitude and gladness.

While he was dressing, a blue-jacket brought a note from the admiral. It invited him to tea on board the warship, with the guests of the SERAPIS. His old friend added that he was coming to lunch with his consul, and wanted time reserved for a long talk. The consul agreed gladly. He was in holiday humor. The day promised to repeat the good moments of the night previous.

At nine o'clock, through the open door of the consulate, Marshall saw Aiken, the wireless operator, signaling from the wharf excitedly to the yacht, and a boat leave the ship and return. Almost immediately the launch, carrying several passengers, again made the trip shoreward.

Half an hour later, Senator Hanley, Miss Cairns, and Livingstone came up the waterfront, and entering the consulate, seated themselves around Marshall's desk. Livingstone was sunk in melancholy. The senator, on the contrary, was smiling broadly. His manner was one of distinct relief. He greeted the consul with hearty good-humor.

"I'm ordered home!" he announced gleefully. Then, remembering the presence of Livingstone, he hastened to add: "I needn't say how sorry I am to give up my yachting trip, but orders are orders. The President," he explained to Marshall, "cables me this morning to come back and take my coat off." The prospect, as a change from playing bridge on a pleasure boat, seemed far from depressing him.

"Those filibusters in the Senate," he continued genially, "are making trouble again. They think they've got me out of the way for another month, but they'll find they're wrong. When that bill comes up, they'll find me at the old stand and ready for business!" Marshall did not attempt to conceal his personal disappointment.

"I am so sorry you are leaving," he said; "selfishly sorry, I mean. I'd hoped you all would be here for several days." He looked inquiringly toward Livingstone.

"I understood the SERAPIS was disabled," he explained.

"She is," answered Hanley. "So's the RALEIGH. At a pinch, the admiral might have stretched the regulations and carried me to Jamaica, but the RALEIGH's engines are knocked about too. I've GOT to reach Kingston Thursday. The German boat leaves there Thursday for New York. At first it looked as though I couldn't do it, but we find that the Royal Mail is due to-day, and she can get to Kingston Wednesday night. It's a great piece of luck. I wouldn't bother you with my troubles," the senator explained pleasantly, "but the agent of the Royal Mail here won't sell me a ticket until you've put your seal to this." He extended a piece of printed paper.

As Hanley had been talking, the face of the consul had grown grave. He accepted the paper, but did not look at it. Instead, he regarded the senator with troubled eyes. When he spoke, his tone was one of genuine concern.

"It is most unfortunate," he said. "But I am afraid the ROYAL MAIL will not take you on board. Because of Las Bocas," he explained. "If we had only known!" he added remorsefully. "It is MOST unfortunate."

"Because of Las Bocas?" echoed Hanley.

"You don't mean they'll refuse to take me to Jamaica because I spent half an hour at the end of a wharf listening to a squeaky gramophone?"

"The trouble," explained Marshall, "is this: if they carried you, all the other passengers would be held in quarantine for ten days, and there are fines to pay, and there would be difficulties over the mails. But," he added hopefully, "maybe the regulations have been altered. I will see her captain, and tell him——"

"See her captain!" objected Hanley. "Why see the captain? He doesn't know I've been to that place. Why tell him? All I need is a clean bill of health from you. That's all HE wants. You have only to sign that paper." Marshall regarded the senator with surprise.

"But I can't," he said.

"You can't? Why not?"

"Because it certifies to the fact that you have not visited Las Bocas. Unfortunately, you have visited Las Bocas."

The senator had been walking up and down the room. Now he seated himself, and stared at Marshall curiously.

"It's like this, Mr. Marshall," he began quietly. "The President desires my presence in Washington, thinks I can be of some use to him there in helping carry out certain party measures—measures to which he pledged himself before his election. Down here, a British steamship line has laid down local rules which, in my case anyway, are ridiculous. The question is, are you going to be bound by the red tape of a ha'penny British colony, or by your oath to the President of the United States?"

The sophistry amused Marshall. He smiled good-naturedly and shook his head.

"I'm afraid, Senator," he said, "that way of putting it is hardly fair. Unfortunately, the question is one of fact. I will explain to the captain——"

"You will explain nothing to the captain!" interrupted Hanley. "This is a matter which concerns no one but our two selves. I am not asking favors of steamboat captains. I am asking an American consul to assist an American citizen in trouble, and," he added, with heavy sarcasm, "incidentally, to carry out the wishes of his President."

Marshall regarded the senator with an expression of both surprise and disbelief.

"Are you asking me to put my name to what is not so?" he said. "Are you serious?"

"That paper, Mr. Marshall," returned Hanley steadily, "is a mere form, a piece of red tape. There's no more danger of my carrying the plague to Jamaica than of my carrying a dynamite bomb. You KNOW that."

"I DO know that," assented Marshall heartily. "I appreciate your position, and I regret it exceedingly. You are the innocent victim of a regulation which is a wise regulation, but which is most unfair to you. My own position," he added, "is not important, but you can believe me, it is not easy. It is certainly no pleasure for me to be unable to help you."

Hanley was leaning forward, his hands on his knees, his eyes watching Marshall closely. "Then you refuse?" he said. "Why?"

Marshall regarded the senator steadily. His manner was untroubled. The look he turned upon Hanley was one of grave disapproval.

"You know why," he answered quietly. "It is impossible."

In sudden anger Hanley rose. Marshall, who had been seated behind his desk, also rose. For a moment, in silence, the two men confronted each other. Then Hanley spoke; his tone was harsh and threatening.

"Then I am to understand," he exclaimed, "that you refuse to carry out the wishes of a United States Senator and of the President of the United States?"

In front of Marshall, on his desk, was the little iron stamp of the consulate. Protectingly, almost caressingly, he laid his hand upon it.

"I refuse," he corrected, "to place the seal of this consulate on a lie."

There was a moment's pause. Miss Cairns, unwilling to remain, and unable to withdraw, clasped her hands unhappily and stared at the floor. Livingstone exclaimed in indignant protest. Hanley moved a step nearer and, to emphasize what he said, tapped his knuckles on the desk. With the air of one confident of his advantage, he spoke slowly and softly.

"Do you appreciate," he asked, "that, while you may be of some importance down here in this fever swamp, in Washington I am supposed to carry some weight? Do you appreciate that I am a senator from a State that numbers four millions of people, and that you are preventing me from serving those people?"

Marshall inclined his head gravely and politely.

"And I want you to appreciate," he said, "that while I have no weight at Washington, in this fever swamp I have the honor to represent eighty millions of people, and as long as that consular sign is over my door I don't intend to prostitute it for YOU, or the President of the United States, or any one of those eighty millions."

Of the two men, the first to lower his eyes was Hanley. He laughed shortly, and walked to the door. There he turned, and indifferently, as though the incident no longer interested him, drew out his watch.

"Mr. Marshall," he said, "if the cable is working, I'll take your tin sign away from you by sunset."

For one of Marshall's traditions, to such a speech there was no answer save silence. He bowed, and, apparently serene and undismayed, resumed his seat. From the contest, judging from the manner of each, it was Marshall, not Hanley, who had emerged victorious.

But Miss Cairns was not deceived. Under the unexpected blow, Marshall had turned older. His clear blue eyes had grown less alert, his broad shoulders seemed to stoop. In sympathy, her own eyes filled with sudden tears.

"What will you do?" she whispered.

"I don't know what I shall do," said Marshall simply. "I should have liked to have resigned. It's a prettier finish. After forty years—to be dismissed by cable is—it's a poor way of ending it."

Miss Cairns rose and walked to the door. There she turned and looked back.

"I am sorry," she said. And both understood that in saying no more than that she had best shown her sympathy.

An hour later the sympathy of Admiral Hardy was expressed more directly.

"If he comes on board my ship," roared that gentleman, "I'll push him down an ammunition hoist and break his damned neck!"

Marshall laughed delightedly. The loyalty of his old friend was never so welcome.

"You'll treat him with every courtesy," he said. "The only satisfaction he gets out of this is to see that he has hurt me. We will not give him that satisfaction."

But Marshall found that to conceal his wound was more difficult than he had anticipated. When, at tea time, on the deck of the war-ship, he again met Senator Hanley and the guests of the SERAPIS, he could not forget that his career had come to an end. There was much to remind him that this was so. He was made aware of it by the sad, sympathetic glances of the women; by their tactful courtesies; by the fact that Livingstone, anxious to propitiate Hanley, treated him rudely; by the sight of the young officers, each just starting upon a career of honor, and possible glory, as his career ended in humiliation; and by the big war-ship herself, that recalled certain crises when he had only to press a button and war-ships had come at his bidding.

At five o'clock there was an awkward moment. The Royal Mail boat, having taken on her cargo, passed out of the harbor on her way to Jamaica, and dipped her colors.

Senator Hanley, abandoned to his fate, observed her departure in silence.

Livingstone, hovering at his side, asked sympathetically: "Have they answered your cable, sir?" "They have," said Hanley gruffly.

"Was it—was it satisfactory?" pursued the diplomat. "It WAS," said the senator, with emphasis.

Far from discouraged, Livingstone continued his inquiries.

"And when," he asked eagerly, "are you going to tell him?"

"Now!" said the senator.

The guests were leaving the ship. When all were seated in the admiral's steam launch, the admiral descended the accommodation ladder and himself picked up the tiller ropes.

"Mr. Marshall," he called, "when I bring the launch broadside to the ship and stop her, you will stand ready to receive the consul's salute."

Involuntarily, Marshall uttered an exclamation of protest. He had forgotten that on leaving the war-ship, as consul, he was entitled to seven guns. Had he remembered, he would have insisted that the ceremony be omitted. He knew that the admiral wished to show his loyalty, knew that his old friend was now paying him this honor only as a rebuke to Hanley. But the ceremony was no longer an honor. Hanley had made of it a mockery. It served only to emphasize what had been taken from him. But, without a scene, it now was too late to avoid it. The first of the seven guns had roared from the bow, and, as often he had stood before, as never he would so stand again, Marshall took his place at the gangway of the launch. His eyes were fixed on the flag, his gray head was uncovered, his hat was pressed above his heart.

For the first time since Hanley had left the consulate, he fell into sudden terror lest he might give way to his emotions. Indignant at the thought, he held himself erect. His face was set like a mask, his eyes were untroubled. He was determined they should not see that he was suffering.

Another gun spat out a burst of white smoke, a stab of flame. There was an echoing roar. Another and another followed. Marshall counted seven, and then, with a bow to the admiral, backed from the gangway.

And then another gun shattered the hot, heavy silence. Marshall, confused, embarrassed, assuming he had counted wrong, hastily returned to his place. But again before he could leave it, in savage haste a ninth gun roared out its greeting. He could not still be mistaken. He turned appealingly to his friend. The eyes of the admiral were fixed upon the war-ship. Again a gun shattered the silence. Was it a jest? Were they laughing at him? Marshall flushed miserably. He gave a swift glance toward the others. They were smiling. Then it was a jest. Behind his back, something of which they all were cognizant was going forward. The face of Livingstone alone betrayed a like bewilderment to his own. But the others, who knew, were mocking him.

For the thirteenth time a gun shook the brooding swamp land of Porto Banos. And then, and not until then, did the flag crawl slowly from the mast-head. Mary Cairns broke the tenseness by bursting into tears. But Marshall saw that every one else, save she and Livingstone, were still smiling. Even the bluejackets in charge of the launch were grinning at him. He was beset by smiling faces. And then from the war-ship, unchecked, came, against all regulations, three long, splendid cheers.

Marshall felt his lips quivering, the warm tears forcing their way to his eyes. He turned beseechingly to his friend. His voice trembled.

"Charles," he begged, "are they laughing at me?"

Eagerly, before the other would answer, Senator Hanley tossed his cigar into the water and, scrambling forward, seized Marshall by the hand.

"Mr. Marshall," he cried, "our President has great faith in Abraham Lincoln's judgment of men. And this salute means that this morning he appointed you our new minister to The Hague. I'm one of those politicians who keeps his word. I TOLD YOU I'd take your tin sign away from you by sunset. I've done it!"